THE FLYING ANGELS

TREASURED HORSES COLLECTION™

titles in Large-Print Editions:

Changing Times

Christmas in Silver Lake

Colorado Summer

The Flying Angels

A Horse for Hannah

Kate's Secret Plan

Louisiana Blue

Pretty Lady of Saratoga

Pride of the Green Mountains

Ride of Courage

Riding School Rivals

Rush for Gold

Spirit of the West

The Stallion of Box Canyon

THE FLYING ANGELS

The story of a vaulter who must overcome her fear to once again perform on her amazing Andalusian

Written by Coleen Hubbard
Illustrated by Sandy Rabinowitz
Cover Illustration by Christa Keiffer
Developed by Nancy Hall, Inc.

Gareth Stevens Publishing
MILWAUKEE

For a free color catalog describing Gareth Stevens' list of high-quality books and multimedia programs, call 1-800-542-2595 (USA) or 1-800-461-9120 (Canada). Gareth Stevens Publishing's Fax: (414) 225-0377.

Library of Congress Cataloging-in-Publication Data

Hubbard, Coleen.
The Flying Angels / written by Coleen Hubbard;
illustrated by Sandy Rabinowitz; cover illustration by Christa Keiffer.
p. cm.
Originally published: Dyersville, Iowa: Ertl Co., 1998.
(Treasured horses collection)
Summary: Adela is excited to perform with the Flying Angels, the
vaulting team to which her sisters belong, but her pride makes
her quit when she falls while dismounting from her horse.
ISBN 0-8368-2401-6 (lib. bdg.)
[1. Horsemanship—Fiction. 2. Horses—Fiction.
3. Pride and vanity—Fiction.] I. Rabinowitz, Sandy, ill.
II. Title. III. Series: Treasured horses collection.
PZ7.H85668Fl   1999
[Fic]—dc21   99-11745

This edition first published in 1999 by
Gareth Stevens Publishing
1555 North RiverCenter Drive, Suite 201
Milwaukee, Wisconsin 53212 USA

© 1998 by Nancy Hall, Inc.
First published by The ERTL Company, Inc., Dyersville, Iowa.

Treasured Horses Collection is a registered trademark of The ERTL Company, Inc.

Printed in the United States of America

1 2 3 4 5 6 7 8 9 03 02 01 00 99

CONTENTS

Adela's First Show

The announcer's voice boomed from the loudspeakers. "Up next in today's vaulting competition will be the Flying Angels from Central Texas."

Outside the Austin Fairgrounds Arena, twelve-year-old Adela Salinas smoothed her shiny black hair for the twentieth time and made sure her thick braid was securely fastened at the end with a white ribbon. Then she adjusted her light blue leotard, exactly like the leotards the other seven girls on her team were wearing.

Adela bounced up and down on the balls of her feet, encased in white, lightweight gymnastic shoes, more from nervousness than from trying to loosen up. This was her first vaulting competition.

Some people said vaulting was just like gymnastics, except it was done on horseback. But that "except" was the most important part of the sport to Adela, because she loved horses more than anything. She especially loved her own horse, an Andalusian named Rio.

Adela had been a vaulter for three years, but she'd been a member of the Central Texas Flying Angels vaulting team for only six months. As the youngest and newest girl on the team, she was made the reserve member, which meant that she did not compete in shows unless one of the first eight girls was injured or ill. Until today, that hadn't happened.

At dinnertime two nights before, Diana, her eldest sister and Number 1 on the team, had gotten a phone call from Emily Bonner's mother. Emily was Number 7 on the Flying Angels.

"Emily's come down with a sore throat," Mrs. Bonner had told Diana. "I'm afraid the competition in Austin is out of the question for her. If it's strep, the doctor said there's no way she'll be able to leave the house for three or four days, at the very least. I've already spoken with your trainer, but Emily wanted me to call you directly, because she feels awful about letting the team down."

"Please tell Emily not to worry, Mrs. Bonner," Diana had said, while her three younger sisters listened intently from their places at the dining room table. "That's why we have a reserve member on the team."

And Diana had smiled across the room at Adela.

"Well, Adela, it sounds like you'll be competing in the show in Austin," Abuelito, the Salinas girls' grandfather, had said cheerfully.

Abuelito lived in the little house behind theirs. He had been Adela's spotter and cheering section since she'd started learning to vault when she was nine.

Adela's mother must have guessed at some of the worries crowding into her youngest daughter's mind, because she'd said, "You'll be fine, honey. You've been practicing with the team for months now. Why, your compulsories are practically perfect."

"Just relax and have fun with it," her father had said. "Does anybody want more steak?"

Adela hadn't wanted any more steak that night. In fact, she'd had butterflies in her stomach almost continuously since then.

Relax and have fun with it, relax and have fun with it . . ., Adela told herself as the Flying Angels waited for the signal to enter the arena.

She almost wished she could go first, instead of

seventh in Emily's spot, because the longer she waited, the more keyed up she knew she'd get.

Adela glanced up the line at her three older sisters: Diana, seventeen years old, was tall and slender, with beautiful wavy hair and one of the best back-salto dismounts Adela had ever seen. At the end of the summer Diana would be leaving the Flying Angels, though. Come fall she would be going to college in Dallas. Adela already missed her like crazy.

Adela's sixteen-year-old sister, Isabel, was in the Number 3 spot on the team. Isabel was shorter and stockier than Diana and very strong, which made her a natural as the base for pairs and threes.

She was a great coach, too. Isabel helped Adela a lot, especially with the Flying Angels' freestyle routines. And that summer she'd been coaching a couple of younger kids who were just starting out in vaulting.

At fourteen, Vicki was closest to Adela in age— maybe that's why they definitely had their moments of rubbing each other the wrong way. Petite and graceful, Vicki was in the Number 5 spot on the team. But in Adela's opinion, she acted as though she was more than ready to replace Diana as Number 1.

Right now Vicki was fidgeting, circling her arms forward and backward, forward and backward, doing mindless last-minute warm-ups.

Adela took a couple of deep breaths herself, hoping to relax a little, and stared at the Flying Angels' vaulting horse standing at the head of the line—a big, chestnut half-Percheron named Charlie. Charlie was patient, steady, and powerful. Adela had practiced on him many times.

Adela wasn't worried about Charlie at all, or about Mr. Conover, the longeur for the Flying Angels who controlled the speed of the vaulting horse. No, what she was worried about was herself. For the first time her vaulting ability would be adding to, or subtracting from, the Flying Angels' total points as a team.

Adela jumped when Allison Martz, the Number 8 vaulter, complained, "What's taking them so long?" She sounded as nervous as Adela felt.

Then the announcer's voice boomed out the words Adela both longed and dreaded to hear: "Ladies and gentlemen, may I proudly present . . . the Central Texas Flying Angels."

It's Show Time

As the Flying Angels' run-in music began to play, Adela took one last deep breath and marked time with the other girls.

"Remember to smile," she told herself.

Leading Charlie, Mr. Conover entered the arena and ran into the riding ring. Behind him was Diana and after her the remaining seven girls, one behind another, moving in step.

Staying in a line, the group trotted completely around the ring, allowing all three judges to take a good look at Charlie's overall fitness and grooming and the turnout of his tack. In a competition, the vaulting horse was rated as well as the vaulters.

Mr. Conover halted Charlie in the center of the ring and faced the senior judge. The rest of the team lined up in a row to Mr. Conover's left, facing the judge as well. They all saluted in unison.

Vaulters 2 through 8 ran to the side of the ring where Mrs. Conover was standing. Diana remained in the middle of the ring with Mr. Conover and Charlie.

After the senior judge had rung a bell, music for the Flying Angels' compulsories swelled from the loudspeakers. Charlie began cantering to the left. It was time for the program to start.

Adela had seen her sisters performing their compulsory exercises hundreds of times, and she'd done them herself thousands of times at home, on her own horse, Rio. Plus she'd practiced them on Charlie at the Conovers' stable, along with the rest of the Flying Angels, for six months.

While the older girls performed the first block of compulsories, Adela replayed them over and over in her own head, imagining herself doing the basic seat, the flag, the mill, and the stand.

The seat, the flag, and the stand were static exercises, which meant the vaulter had to be fully balanced and hold a position for at least four of the horse's strides. Adela was pretty sure she would not have trouble with any of those. The mill, though, was dynamic. It involved motion, and the judges gave points for speed, height, and push-off.

Adela was concerned about how well she would do the mill, the scissors, and the flank—the dynamic exercises in the second block of the compulsories—not to mention the vault-ons and dismounts. Each vault-on or dismount presented more opportunities to mess up and disgrace both herself and her team.

A round of applause broke into Adela's thoughts. She focused on the riding ring in time to see her sister Isabel completing her dismount, landing with her knees bent, arms outstretched, eyes straight ahead, and a smile on her face.

Sara Palmer, the Number 4 vaulter, ran out to Charlie along the longe line, and vaulted on easily. Only three girls to go before it would be Adela's turn.

Applause for Sara. More applause for Vicki. The time for her own performance came all too quickly. Mrs. Conover tapped her on her shoulder, and Adela took her first running steps onto the soft sand of the riding ring. From the grandstands behind her, a voice called out, "Do it just like at home, on Rio!"

Adela recognized Abuelito's voice. Because Adela's parents often had to work Saturdays at their insurance firm, they rarely got a chance to see their daughters' shows. But Abuelito never missed a single performance. Not only was he the girls' biggest fan, but it was Abuelito who had bought Rio as a surprise for Adela for her twelfth birthday, from a retired vaulter in West Texas.

Adela waited behind Mr. Conover until Martha Woller, the Number 6 vaulter, had swung herself off Charlie in a dismount. Then Adela passed under the whip that Mr. Conover held in his right hand and sprinted down the longe line he held in his left. She ran in step with the cantering horse and took hold of the grips on the vaulting saddle, called a surcingle.

Grasping the grips tightly, she quickly sprang forward with both of her feet. Using Charlie's forward motion to thrust her back and up, Adela spread her legs, with her left leg continuing to point straight down at the ground and her right leg swinging skyward.

Adela pushed with her arms at the same time, lifting herself higher and higher in the air, until her body was parallel to Charlie's back, and her right leg was extended above her. As her right leg swung down slowly, Adela continued to push against the grips to make sure she had a soft landing. She ended up in the correct spot on Charlie's broad back.

Next, the three judges would be judging Adela's basic seat, marking her for balance and suppleness.

For four of Charlie's cantering strides, Adela sat in the center of his back with her arms held straight out to the sides and her upper body perfectly still. No defaults yet, she told herself, lowering her arms.

Holding onto the grips of the surcingle again, Adela swung both of her legs forward and then backward, pushing herself upward and landing gently with her toes on Charlie's back. She lowered immediately into a kneeling position.

Supported by her left leg, which she crossed over Charlie's back, and her right hand, still holding onto the grips, Adela raised her right leg and her left arm in the air at the same time and held them there for four strides. Then she went back to a seat astride.

No problems so far, Adela told herself.

Next came the stand, Adela's favorite exercise, and one she was always good at. Adela swung herself into the kneeling position again on Charlie's back. Still holding onto the grips, she jumped up into a crouch. She turned loose of the surcingle and brought her upper body straight up, until she was standing erect.

Adela gazed straight ahead and extended her hands out to the sides for a good five strides, before lowering herself again into the seat astride.

If performed correctly, the mill was supposed to

make the audience think of an old-fashioned windmill. It involved a complete rotation on the horse's back in a sitting position, done in four phases, with each phase lasting four canter strides.

Adela knew the judges would fault her for missing a beat, so she counted to herself as she lifted her right leg over Charlie's neck, then closed both legs on the horse's left side for four strides. She lifted her left leg all the way over Charlie's back, until she was sitting astride him again, but facing his tail for four strides. Then her right leg lifted over his rump, joining her left leg on Charlie's right side. Adela returned to the basic seat and swung into a simple dismount on Charlie's left side. As she touched down on the soft sand of the ring, Adela didn't have to remember to smile.

She broke into a huge grin, enjoying the thunder of applause from the audience as she left the ring, while Number 8, Allison Martz, took over.

"Great job, Adela!" Mrs. Conover congratulated her when she reached the sidelines.

Diana patted Adela on the back and gave her the thumbs-up sign.

Adela, though pretty satisfied with her performance, knew she still had plenty of hard work ahead of her—the scissors and the flank were the two most difficult exercises in the compulsories. But her confidence as a vaulter was growing.

I did it! Adela told herself. I've proved myself as a Flying Angel.

Even though Diana would be leaving for college soon, there would still be three Salinas girls as regular members of the Central Texas Flying Angels, Adela thought with satisfaction.

Nobody's Perfect

Adela's teammates clustered around her and praised her to the skies. Even Vicki said, "You looked excellent out there, Dell. A real pro."

Adela was raring to go on the last two exercises in the compulsory program. Nothing could stop her now.

When it was her turn, she breezed through the four phases of the scissors, which was a lot like the mill in that the vaulter rotated completely around on the horse. But the scissors was performed with the body as well as the legs swinging into the air.

Adela didn't miss a beat. Landing squarely in the seat astride after completing the scissors, she began the last of her compulsory exercises—the flank.

The flank was made up of two phases. In the first, the vaulter swings into a handstand on the horse's back and then glides down slowly with both legs on the horse's left side, until she settles into a side seat.

In the second phase, the vaulter swings her body up in the air again, straightening out over the horse's back as if she were about to perform a second handstand. But instead she pushes herself away from the grips and plants her feet firmly on the ground, on the far side of the horse.

During this second phase, about halfway through the exercise, Adela was sitting sideways on Charlie and telling herself that in just a few moments she would have aced her first-ever competitive compulsories. She had plenty to be proud about.

Adela took a deep breath and pushed herself into the final upswing of the flank. But before her body was nearly high enough in the air, her right hand slipped off the grip.

With no time to adjust, her left wrist collapsed beneath her weight. Adela fell forward, crashing full length onto Charlie's broad, sweaty back. As her face jammed into the bottom of his mane, there was a loud gasp from the audience.

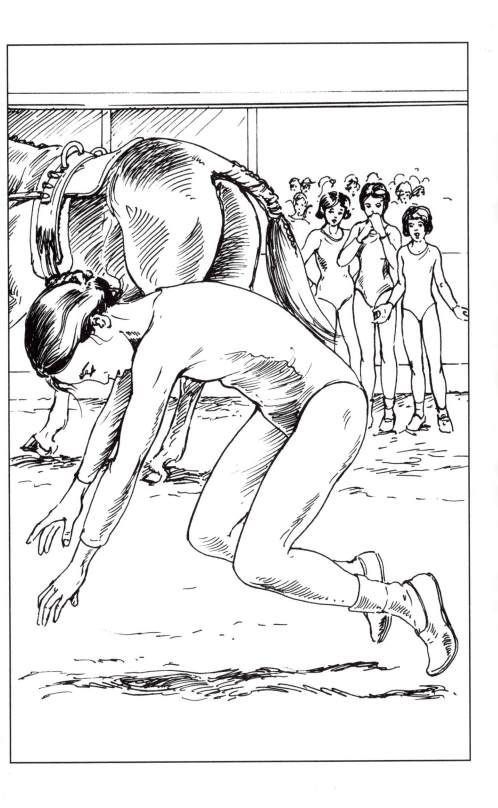

For a few seconds, Adela just lay there, clutching the surcingle with both hands. Should she attempt to finish the flank exercise? Should she vault off?

Mr. Conover was slowing Charlie down. Adela knew he was concerned that she might slip sideways and end up underneath the horse's hooves.

Gritting her teeth, she pushed herself up into a seat astride. She took hold of the grips again and attempted a simple dismount. But when her feet touched the sand of the riding ring, she bobbled and fell to her knees.

Lifting herself up off the ground, sand sticking to her face and hair, Adela saw her sisters staring wide-eyed at her from the sidelines. From the grandstands, she heard giggling over the sound of the Flying Angels' music.

Charlie was continuing a slow canter around the ring. Behind Mr. Conover, Allison Martz waited for her turn to begin.

Adela scrambled to her feet and ran out of the ring as fast as she could, her face burning with embarrassment.

When Adela joined the rest of the team on the sidelines, Diana tried to put her arm around her little sister's shoulders.

Adela shrugged it off. She didn't deserve any

comforting, especially not from the Number 1 vaulter, a Salinas who never made mistakes.

"In my first show, I landed flat on my face on my dismount," Isabel told Adela. Adela shook her head. She didn't remember any such thing.

Even Vicki tried to make Adela feel better.

"So you lost a few points at the end. Everything else you did was okay," Vicki said.

"These kinds of experiences are all part of growing as a vaulter," Mrs. Conover said. "I know you'll shine in the team kur this afternoon."

The kur was the five-minute-long, freestyle part of the competition. All eight team members participated in a flowing sequence of singles, pairs, and threes set to music.

Adela shook her head. She knew what she had to do. She'd already made up her mind.

"Mrs. Conover, I'd just foul up everybody in the freestyle. I'm resigning from the team," she said.

"Adela, don't decide that now. You're too upset," said Mrs. Conover.

"You're part of the team, Adela!" Isabel said. "Think about the rest of us."

"Yeah, we'll lose points if all eight of us don't participate in the kur," Vicki added disapprovingly. "You'll be letting the team down."

"The judges will take only a few points off if there are seven girls instead of eight," Adela said. "But they'll take a ton of points off if I blow it again this afternoon."

"You won't blow it, Adela," Diana said. "Have a little bit of faith in yourself."

Adela shook her head, tears burning her eyes. She didn't care what her sister or Mrs. Conover said. They were just being kind. She knew the truth. She knew she didn't belong on the team with the others.

She hoped she wouldn't start blubbering and embarrass herself further. Before anyone else could argue with her, Adela walked quickly toward the exit from the arena.

"Adela, you're acting like a big baby!" Vicki said in a loud voice.

"You'll change your mind once you've thought about this!" Isabel called after her.

I won't! Adela told herself.

She jogged out of the building, aiming for the parking lot where her granddad's truck was parked.

She was dodging around fair-goers when she heard Abuelito's voice calling after her: "Adela, slow down! It's hard to run in cowboy boots."

When he caught up with her and wrapped her in a big, warm hug, she let herself burst into tears.

"I know, I know," Abuelito said soothingly, stroking her hair. "Let me see that left wrist."

Adela hadn't even thought about the wrist that had buckled under her in the ring. Now she realized that it was painful for her to bend it.

"Yep, it's a little swollen," Abuelito said, touching her wrist gently. "First we'll buy a bag of ice to stick that sprained wrist into, and then we'll get you home."

"What about Diana and Isabel and Vicki?" Adela asked, wiping tears away with her right hand.

"They can catch a ride back to San Antonio with the Conovers. I'll pick them up at the stable later this afternoon," Abuelito said.

"I'm never doing this again!" Adela said after Abuelito had opened the passenger door of his truck and helped her climb in.

"What! You're never going to vault again?" said Abuelito, pulling out of the parking lot. "I can't believe that. You love it, and you've worked so hard at it. And what about Rio? He'll get bored with nothing to do but stand around in the paddock."

"Rio and I will think of something else to do," Adela said. "Maybe I'll start jumping on him. Or learn dressage."

"Well, you could do that, too," said her grandfather. "Andalusians are certainly versatile."

Abuelito was right. Andalusians were good at lots of different things. Adela knew that Andalusians were counted among the most graceful, athletic, and beautiful horses in the world. Because of their agility and calm temperaments, they were favorite horses for the circus, as well as for parades and demonstrations.

In fact, with their strong, athletic bodies, tremendous endurance, and remarkable intelligence, there was almost nothing that Andalusians couldn't do well.

And so even though Rio was an excellent vaulting horse, Adela was sure he would make an equally good jumper or dressage horse.

Thinking about Rio helped Adela forget her painful wrist, now packed in a bag of crushed ice. But she was certain that her foul-up in Austin would remain fresh in her mind for a long, long time.

Rio

When Adela and Abuelito turned onto the gravel road that led across the Salinases' ten acres on the outskirts of San Antonio, Rio was the first thing Adela saw.

The big gray horse was grazing in the large front paddock, along with Adela's sisters' horses, Boots and Nina. As soon as Rio heard the truck, he raised his beautiful head to nicker a greeting. Then he galloped alongside the paddock fence, easily keeping up with Adela and Abuelito as they drove toward the houses.

The main house, a low, sprawling white stucco, had a red tile roof and a green ceramic fountain out front for the birds that nested in the surrounding oak trees. Behind the main house was the small, square house where Abuelito lived.

Beyond Abuelito's house was the barn, with four stalls and a tack room. Beside the barn was the Salinases' riding ring and the two practice barrels where Adela—as well as her sisters—had learned to vault.

Each barrel was made of oil drums welded together and covered with strips of carpeting to protect the vaulters. The barrels stood on four iron legs that raised them about sixteen hands in the air, the approximate height of a horse. Two handles were fixed to each practice barrel, just like the grips on a vaulting surcingle.

Adela had put in more hours on those barrels

than she could have counted, trying every move, even inventing a few. As she looked at the barrels from the front seat of the truck, she thought of all those hours, all culminating in the awful embarrassment of the competition in Austin.

Before she could descend into gloom, Rio stuck his head over the fence and nickered again. Adela couldn't resist him. She climbed out of the truck and walked over to say hello.

Rio was a little over sixteen hands high, his color a warm, velvety gray, with a long, flowing mane and tail. He had small ears, pricked toward Adela at the moment, and large, intelligent, dark brown eyes set wide apart.

He stretched his neck out to sniff at Adela's hair with his soft, dark gray nose. Then he nibbled at her braid.

Adela laughed. "Cut it out, Rio," she said, pushing his nose away. "I'll bring you a carrot from the house."

Abuelito kept a plastic bag full of carrots in his refrigerator for Rio and the other horses. When Adela walked through the back door of his little house to take some, the photos on the wall caught her eye: Diana, Isabel, and Vicki doing threes on Charlie at a show, Isabel and Vicki practicing pairs at home on Boots, Diana at the Spring Classic in El Paso, winning a gold on Nina for her individual freestyle.

And there was a new photograph of herself that Adela hadn't seen yet. The picture showed her on Rio performing the flank, just about ready to vault off on Rio's far side. A look of total concentration was on her face.

She studied it carefully before murmuring, "I can't believe it. My form is perfect in this photo."

Adela sighed, turning her back on the pictures and opening the refrigerator door. So what if I can do it perfectly during practice? What counts is being able to perform under pressure, and that's where I'm a flop, she said to herself. It was time to face up to facts. She didn't have what it took to be a member of the Flying Angels. She had better put it behind her and move on.

At dinner that evening, Adela stuck to her guns, even though her sisters tried hard to argue her out of her decision.

Diana said, "Adela, you're a gifted vaulter. You're already a lot more advanced than I was at your age."

Isabel went on, "Nobody can ever be perfect, Adela. And don't forget that this was your first competition, which put a lot of pressure on you."

"That's still not an excuse for quitting," Vicki muttered. She turned to Diana and said, "I told you she was too immature for the team."

"I'm not being immature. I'm being logical!" Adela said heatedly. "The Flying Angels won a silver after I resigned. If I'd stayed in, the team wouldn't have won anything!"

Mr. Salinas said, "This is Adela's decision. Even if we all don't agree with it, let's please respect it."

And the girls' mother said, "Have you forgotten that Adela's wrist was sprained? She couldn't have competed anyway."

Adela's wrist did hurt. But deep down she knew that if she had really wanted to compete in the kur, she could have bandaged it and participated. On the other hand, if she had gone out, she'd have only made the whole team look amateurish.

It was over and done with, as her granddad would say.

The next morning Abuelito helped Adela set up a series of trotting poles behind the barn so that she could start her jumping lessons. They had not been out there long when they heard a car crunching along the gravel road.

"Who could that be?" Abuelito said.

Adela followed her granddad around the barn, in time to see a long green car pulling up beside the main house.

Isabel walked out on the front porch and down the steps to greet the three people getting out of the car: a large light-haired man in a gray suit, a small woman wearing a lime-green blouse and matching plaid skirt, and a girl who looked as if she was around Vicki's age.

The girl was small and slender, with delicate features, and pale blonde hair that she'd gathered into a knot at the back of her neck. She was wearing a pink T-shirt and shorts and carrying a white gym bag.

Though Adela didn't recognize them at all, Isabel was acting very friendly, shaking hands with each of them. Then Vicki came out of the house to say hi to them, too.

Isabel caught sight of Abuelito and Adela, and she waved them forward. "Mr. and Mrs. McFarland, Daphne, this is my youngest sister, Adela, and our granddad, Mr. Montalvo."

"Pleased to meet you," said Mr. McFarland, shaking hands with them both.

By way of explanation, Mrs. McFarland added, "We were in the audience at the vaulting competition in Austin yesterday."

Adela felt her face getting hot all over again.

"Daphne is a natural gymnast," Mrs. McFarland continued, "and she wants desperately to try vaulting."

The blond girl smiled in a noncommittal way.

"So we spoke with the Conovers about it," Mr. McFarland said, "and they told us that they had no time to spare at the moment. They suggested that we approach Isabel after the show about coaching Daphne."

"Isabel very graciously agreed, so here we are," said Mrs. McFarland.

Adela stared at her middle sister. Why hadn't Isabel said anything to her about it?

"Daphne, do you want to change into your leotard?" asked Vicki. "Come on in. I'll show you where to go."

Daphne followed her up the front steps and into the house.

Isabel turned to Daphne's parents. "I'll show you our riding ring and practice barrels."

The three of them set off down the gravel road in the direction of the barn.

After everyone had left, Adela and her granddad looked at each other.

"Abuelito, did you know about this?" Adela asked him.

He shook his head. "But I think it's good that Isabel is taking on students. It means she's serious about her coaching," he said.

"I guess so," said Adela.

But she was thinking about Daphne McFarland already being a gymnast. If she had all the moves down, it shouldn't take long for her to become a vaulter. Was it possible Adela's sisters were already shopping for her replacement?

Adela didn't have a chance to talk to Isabel alone. But once Daphne had hurried over to the barn in a light blue leotard—which just happened to be very close to the Flying Angels' color—Adela cornered Vicki.

"Why didn't you guys tell me about this?" Adela asked her youngest sister.

Vicki shrugged. "Isabel thought you were too upset about the competition to want to hear anything more about vaulting, that's all," she said. "It's no big deal."

So maybe it wasn't.

But when Adela climbed onto the paddock fence and watched Daphne vault onto one of their practice barrels, her sinking feeling returned.

Daphne McFarland was *good*.

With just a few minutes coaching from Isabel, she was able to take hold of the handles and mount the practice barrel straight into a handstand. To make matters even worse, Daphne did a flank perfectly, as

though she'd been doing it for years. Then she did a leapfrog dismount.

"That's amazing, Daphne!" Adela heard Vicki say.

"It's pretty simple, really. Don't forget, I've been doing gymnastics since I was five," said Daphne brightly. "Want me to demonstrate that dismount again?"

"Sure!" said Vicki. "Then I'll show you more of the vaulting compulsories."

Adela felt Rio nibbling at her braid, and she turned to rub his head. Then she jumped off the fence and headed toward the barn to grab a halter.

It's nothing to me if Daphne's great at vaulting or not, Adela told herself. I'm going to work Rio on the trotting poles.

CHAPTER FIVE

Adela Makes an Offer

Daphne McFarland was the last person Adela felt like talking about at the dinner table that evening. Which was too bad, because Daphne was the main topic of conversation for Adela's sisters.

Even Diana had something to say.

She'd been shopping for clothes for college that day. But she'd driven back home before the McFarlands left, just in time to see the end of a freestyle routine Daphne had been able to scrape together.

"She has plenty of energy and strength on the practice barrel," Diana said. "I was impressed."

Vicki was really enthusiastic about all the

different moves Daphne could do. She told their parents, "Daphne does roll mounts and clip dismounts. She can even do a handstand roll-under to belly lie."

"She sounds very talented," their father said, passing around a platter of corn-on-the-cob.

"And Daphne's light as a feather. She'd make a great flyer," said Isabel. Adela sensed she was eager to try pairs with Daphne.

"Daphne's going to teach me how to mount into a shoulder hang," said Vicki, helping herself to corn.

"I have a feeling she'll end up coaching us, instead of the other way around," said Isabel.

Abuelito cleared his throat. When he had everyone's attention, he asked, "Has anyone seen Daphne on a horse yet?"

"No," Isabel answered. "Today we stuck to the practice barrel because I wanted to see how advanced her moves were before we added a horse to the mix."

"She's only thirteen and a half, but she can do stuff we've never even heard of!" said Vicki.

"Daphne's coming back tomorrow afternoon. I'll put her on Nina then," Isabel said to their granddad.

"How long has Daphne been riding?" asked their mother, taking a hot roll from the bread basket.

Isabel shrugged. "I didn't ask her," she said. All of the Salinas girls had ridden since they were toddlers. Isabel just assumed that Daphne was as comfortable around horses as they were.

The next morning Adela rode Rio over the trot-poles. He was so good at maneuvering through the course that Adela and Abuelito decided to start him on low jumps in a few days.

"I'm sure the Conovers would lend us a couple of their collapsible jumps," Abuelito said to his granddaughter. "Why don't we drive over to their stable this afternoon, and . . ."

But Adela interrupted. "Uh . . . I thought I'd bathe Rio this afternoon. You know how much he enjoys it."

Rio did love to be bathed. He even liked having his mane shampooed. But Adela's real reason for bathing Rio was that she wanted to stick around to watch Daphne McFarland vault on Nina.

Mr. McFarland dropped Daphne off at the barn at around four, just as the hot summer afternoon started to cool off a little.

Adela had already laid out all of her grooming supplies on the bench outside the barn, and she was spraying Rio off with a hose.

"When should I pick Daphne up?" Adela heard Mr. McFarland ask Isabel.

"Six o'clock will be fine," Isabel told him.

Mr. McFarland rolled away down the gravel road, leaving Daphne with Isabel and Vicki.

Daphne was wearing the light blue leotard again and white gymnastic shoes just like Adela's vaulting shoes.

"Shall I go over to the practice barrels?" Daphne said to Isabel brightly.

"No, I think we'll start you on Nina today," Isabel replied.

"Nina?" Daphne said. She seemed puzzled, and looked around as if trying to figure out who Nina could possibly be.

"Nina's our horse," Isabel explained, smiling. She pointed through the side door of the barn. "Right now she's in her stall."

"Oh," Daphne said in a flat voice. Adela thought she suddenly looked apprehensive.

"I'll show you how to tack her up," said Vicki, walking toward the door.

"I forgot to ask you, Daphne," Isabel said over her shoulder as she followed Vicki. "How long have you been riding?"

"I—uh—I've ridden . . . um . . . once or twice," Daphne said.

The two Salinas girls stopped dead and turned

around. "Once or twice?" Vicki repeated.

"Is that important?" said Daphne, looking back at the practice barrels, her face full of longing. "I figured the horse was sort of automatic."

"The horse is only the most important part of vaulting," Adela murmured to herself.

But she heard Vicki saying, "The horse is kind of automatic."

Adela had the feeling that if Daphne had said, "I'd be happier on a dirt bike," Vicki would have agreed with her.

Even Isabel said, "Maybe knowing how to ride isn't as much of an issue as tuning into the rhythm of the horse. And with your balance and coordination, Daphne . . ."

"It'll be a piece of cake for you," Vicki told Daphne.

Adela switched off the sprayer. If Daphne hadn't come to vaulting through an interest in horses, then she had a question for her. "How did you get to know about vaulting, Daphne?" she asked.

"My cousin Meredith is a vaulter," Daphne said. "She's Number 1 vaulter on a team called the Tyler High-Flyers in East Texas."

Adela understood that. She'd gotten into vaulting herself because of how amazing her older sisters had looked, performing all kinds of incredible feats on the back of a cantering horse.

"Have you ever heard of the High-Flyers?" Daphne asked Vicki.

Vicki nodded. "They did really well at the competition in Houston last spring," she said.

"My parents and I went to Houston that weekend to see Meredith," Daphne said. "She looked so cool that I decided I wanted to try it myself. I can't wait to be on a vaulting team."

Like the Flying Angels, maybe? Adela thought.

Adela's sisters and Daphne walked into the barn to introduce Daphne to Nina. Adela was tempted to follow them, but Rio nudged Adela with his nose, as if to say, "I've been waiting patiently for a shampoo. Are you giving me one, or not?"

Adela had already finished shampooing and rinsing Rio's mane and was working on his tail before the three girls came out of the barn again with Nina.

The bay mare was tacked up—backpad, vaulting surcingle, and bridle. Daphne was leading her, although the blonde girl didn't look very happy about it. With almost every step Nina took, Daphne glanced down at the mare's hooves, as though she was convinced her own toes were about to be squashed.

Did she think someone else would handle the

horse part for her, and she'd just concentrate on her moves? Adela wondered.

Isabel walked on Nina's far side, carrying the longe whip. Vicki held the longe line.

"Lead her right into the ring," Isabel said to Daphne.

Adela moved Rio around so that she could groom him without missing anything that went on during the vaulting lesson.

Isabel attached the longe line to the center ring of Nina's nosepiece. Vicki stood behind her as she started the mare moving to the left.

"We'll begin at a walk," Isabel called out to Daphne, who was waiting outside the ring. She nodded. She seemed nervous and edgy.

"Vicki, show Daphne a simple mount, okay?" Isabel said.

"You'll walk down the longe line in step with the horse," Vicki told Daphne as she walked down the right side of the longe line. She walked alongside Nina for a couple of seconds before she reached out for the grips.

"Correct position for a vaulter who is ready to mount is even with the surcingle," Isabel told Daphne, "not in front or behind it. As the horse's left front foot steps forward, jump forward with both of your feet

43

well ahead of the surcingle. The movement of the horse will thrust you back and up."

Vicki jumped, and Nina's forward motion moved Vicki's body back and up. Vicki spread her legs, pushed with her arms, and swung up and over Nina's back.

"It's a lot harder for the vaulter at a walk," Vicki pointed out to her sister. "You really have to push. Why don't you start Daphne at a trot?"

"That's okay," Daphne said quickly. "I'm strong enough to push myself up."

"We'll do a trot as soon as she gets used to Nina," Isabel told Vicki. To Daphne, Isabel added, "Always lower yourself down gently. If you thump down too hard, you can bruise the horse's back."

As Nina circled, Vicki next showed Daphne the basic seat, her arms held straight out to the sides. Then Vicki swung off the horse, landing on the inside with her knees bent and her arms out.

"Okay, your turn, Daphne," Isabel said.

Daphne hesitated on the sidelines, until Vicki said, "I'll be spotting for you."

Vicki motioned Daphne forward to a position behind Isabel and joined her there, while Nina continued walking in a circle to the left.

"Move down the longe line in step with the horse,

Daphne," Isabel directed. "Count the beats out loud if it will help."

Adela could see Daphne's lips moving. She could also see how pale the girl's face was. She looked anxious and unhappy.

She didn't move forward until Vicki gave her a little push. Then Daphne walked down the longe line toward Nina.

The closer Daphne got to the mare, the shorter her strides became, until she was practically taking baby steps. She couldn't stop altogether, because Vicki was almost treading on her heels.

"Reach out and take hold of the grips," Isabel called to Daphne.

Daphne reached out cautiously, but she was glancing down at the ground again. She was probably wondering how much it would hurt to have one of Nina's big hooves mashing down on her lightweight gymnastic shoes.

Vicki ended up placing Daphne's hands on the grips herself. "One, two . . ." Vicki counted. "Okay, jump!"

Daphne hopped, and Vicki boosted the girl's left leg off the ground.

To avoid crashing against the horse's side, Daphne had to swing her right leg up and over Nina's

back. But she was so tense that she landed stiffly on the backpad, with a thud that annoyed Nina.

The bay mare wasn't used to inexperienced vaulters. And she wasn't the most easy-going animal even on a good day. Nina twitched her tail angrily.

Daphne clung to the grips of the vaulting surcingle and stared down at her mount while Nina plodded around the circle, her ears flattened with irritation.

Isabel called out, "You're doing fine, Daphne. I think I'll try you on Boots, though. He's a steadier horse, with years of vaulting practice behind him."

Adela knew that Isabel didn't want the Salinases' main vaulting horse to go sour on them due to Daphne's inexperience.

Daphne just nodded, but Adela saw her cheeks blush a bright red. She wasn't looking good, and she realized it.

Daphne probably wasn't used to ever being physically awkward. Mr. McFarland had called his daughter a natural gymnast, and Adela believed him.

Adela was beginning to feel sorry for the girl. After her own fiasco in Austin, she knew very well what it was like to feel out of control on a horse with everyone watching intently.

Then Adela noticed that Rio was watching the

vaulting with interest and fidgeting as though he
wanted to get into the ring.

Impulsively, Adela turned off the hose and called
out to Isabel, "Boots can be awfully rough for a first
timer, Isabel. Why not try Daphne on Rio?"

CHAPTER SIX

Daphne and Rio

Isabel brought Nina to a halt and answered from the riding ring, "Thanks, Adela!" She sounded surprised. "It won't be for long," she added, "just until Daphne gets used to the rhythms."

"That's a good idea, Adela," said Abuelito, who had walked up behind her. "I think this guy misses his vaulting practice anyway." He patted Rio on the neck.

Now that Nina was standing still, Daphne did a nice push-away dismount. Once she was on the ground, she put as much space between herself and the bay mare as she could.

Vicki unhooked Nina from the longe line, and then she trotted the horse over to the spot where

Adela and Rio were standing with Abuelito.

"I'll get some towels to dry Rio off," Vicki said.

She handed Abuelito Nina's reins and hurried into the barn as if she were afraid Adela might change her mind about lending Rio.

Isabel started untacking the bay mare, while Daphne hung back. She seemed to be sizing up Adela's horse.

"He's beautiful," she said to Adela. She reached out gingerly to stroke Rio's shoulder a couple of times. "Is he a special breed?"

Adela nodded. "Rio's an Andalusian. Andalusians have been bred in Spain for centuries," she told Daphne. "Rio belonged to a vaulter who retired. Abuelito bought him for my twelfth birthday."

"Lucky you," said Daphne.

Abuelito added, "Andalusians are wonderful horses, very calm and steady."

Adela knew her granddad had said this so that Daphne might feel comfortable around Rio. It seemed to have worked. Adela watched as Daphne edged a little closer to the big gray horse, and even stroked his cheek.

"He seems nice," Daphne said.

"He's a good guy," said Adela fondly.

Vicki came out of the barn carrying a couple of old beach towels. She briskly rubbed down a few of Rio's damper spots, and the blazing hot Texas sun dried the rest of him in no time at all.

Isabel placed the backpad and surcingle on the Andalusian and tightened the buckles. Adela slipped on his bridle.

"Ready to go?" Isabel said to Daphne.

"Ready," said Daphne.

Perhaps Daphne felt more secure about the Andalusian because of what Abuelito had said to her. Or perhaps the two of them just naturally hit it off. Whatever the reason, the second half of Daphne's vaulting lesson was much more relaxed and effective than the first had been.

"Let's try this at a trot," Daphne said to Isabel as soon as Rio began to circle.

She seemed to trust Rio not to step on her. Without hesitating, she moved up close to him and grabbed the grips for the vault-on.

Vicki trotted behind Daphne to help if she needed it. But with the additional pushing power of Rio in a trot, Daphne had no trouble mounting on her own.

After a few simple vault-ons and some basic dismounts, Daphne attempted a roll mount like the one she'd done on the practice barrel. She managed it well.

"That was excellent, Daphne!" Isabel called out.

Suddenly Adela felt a twinge of uneasiness. Or was it just plain jealousy?

Here it was Daphne's first day of vaulting on a real horse, and she was already doing moves that Adela hadn't mastered yet.

Adela felt even more uneasy when Daphne ran over to her at the end of the lesson, and said, "Thanks so much for letting me use him, Adela. I'd love to continue practicing on him until my dad finds me a horse. Would that be okay?"

That could take months! Adela thought. She stared at her two sisters, flabbergasted.

Isabel looked as surprised as Adela, but Vicki said, "How about it, Adela? Can Daphne count on using Rio for a while? You're not vaulting on him."

Even if Adela had no plans to vault on Rio herself, she wanted to start his training as a jumper. If she refused Daphne the use of her horse for her lessons now, though, she'd sound selfish.

Vicki might accuse her of being jealous of Daphne. And Rio did enjoy working in the ring.

"All right," she said to Daphne. "You can practice on him, but just until you get your own horse."

"It might not even have to take that long," Isabel said. "As soon as Daphne has a little more experience, she'll feel more sure of herself, and she'll be able to practice on Nina. Right, Daphne?"

"Uh, right," Daphne said. "But I'd really prefer to

stick with Rio. He's so calm that I almost forget I'm vaulting on an animal."

What is he then? Adela wanted to say. A big piece of gymnastics equipment?!

Daphne certainly overlooked the fact that Rio was a living, breathing being when it came time to cool him down after their session in the riding ring. She left Isabel holding the Andalusian's reins while she and Vicki ran to the practice barrels.

"I'll show you a couple of new moves!" Adela heard Daphne say to her sister.

"What about cooling Rio down?" Adela said to Isabel.

Isabel said, "Daphne hasn't been around horses enough to know any better."

Adela took the reins from Isabel and said, "Never mind. I'll walk him around."

"Thanks, Adela. I definitely owe you," Isabel said.

She headed over to the practice barrels, too. She obviously didn't want to miss out on whatever Daphne was showing Vicki. It seemed to Adela that her entire family was under Daphne's spell.

Abuelito stepped out of the barn and loosened the girth on Rio's vaulting surcingle. He and Adela walked the horse around until Rio's skin felt cool to the touch, and there was no longer any danger that his muscles might stiffen up.

Then they pulled off the surcingle and backpad and turned the Andalusian into the paddock.

"After all that bathing, the first thing he wants to do is roll, naturally," said Adela, smiling.

She and Abuelito watched Rio collapse to his knees and stretch out on his side, then roll over onto his back.

"You know what I think?" Abuelito said to his granddaughter as they watched him. "I think Rio may not be the only one who misses vaulting."

"Well . . ." Adela shrugged. "I'm not a Flying Angel any longer."

"Who said anything about the Flying Angels?" her grandfather replied. "There are probably thousands of vaulters who never compete at a show. They vault because it improves their balance in jumping or dressage and keeps them in shape for riding. Or they do it just for fun."

He gazed at his granddaughter and added, "You enjoy it too much to give it up, don't you, Adela?"

Adela looked over at the practice barrels, where Daphne was coaching Isabel and Vicki while they did mounts into arabesques.

Yes, she had to admit. She'd like to try that move herself.

CHAPTER
SEVEN

Daphne Takes Over

"**A**re you sure you don't want to come with us and watch, at least?" Diana asked Adela before she, Isabel, and Vicki squeezed into her yellow Volkswagen to drive to the Conovers' stable. The Salinas sisters were off to a practice meet with the rest of the Flying Angels.

"No thanks," Adela said. Since that disastrous day in Austin when she'd quit the team, she hadn't seen any of the other Flying Angels, and she wasn't quite sure she was ready to.

But it wasn't just embarrassment that kept her from going along with her sisters. She also wanted to get back into vaulting, and it was best to do that when the others were away. Even if she only vaulted at home, at least that was better than not vaulting at all.

Adela waved goodbye to her sisters as the car pulled away. Then, as soon as they had disappeared in a cloud of gravel dust, she hurried over to her granddad's little house.

"Abuelito?" Adela said, pushing open his screen door. "Are you busy?"

Her grandfather was repairing some reins in his living room. "What can I do for you, Adela?" he asked, laying the reins down on the coffee table.

"I want to try some vaults on Rio, and I could use a longeur," she said.

"I thought you'd never ask!" said Abuelito.

Adela limbered up while Abuelito tacked up Rio. Then they led the Andalusian into the riding ring.

Adela had replayed the image of herself slipping and falling to her knees at the competition so many times that she felt a bit tentative. What if she never got her vaulting rhythm back?

Her grandfather must have realized she was feeling unsure of herself, because he said, "Let's start out simple, Adela—simple mount, basic seat, then maybe a flag and a stand."

Adela noticed he hadn't mentioned a flank, or even a mill. Those more challenging moves might be a long time off, she told herself sadly.

Abuelito signaled Rio with the whip, and the horse began to canter to the left. His small alert ears were pricked forward; his long tail was arched and proud; his gait was smooth and easy. Adela waited until her horse had made one complete circle. Then she ran down the longe line in step with Rio. She reached out for the grips, jumped forward, swung herself high into the air, and lowered herself gently into a seat astride.

"Very nice, Adela!" Abuelito said encouragingly.

Adela counted a couple of strides. Then she turned loose of the grips and stretched her arms out to the sides. After four strides she felt so relaxed and comfortable that she raised her left leg in the air and held onto her ankle in the "ballerina" seat.

"You did that perfectly!" Abuelito called out approvingly.

Adela smiled and did a flag. She extended her left arm and her right leg and held them perfectly straight.

Then she did a limp flag, taking the same position, but lying crossways on Rio's back.

She did a basic stand for ten whole strides.

Then she lowered herself into the "killer," holding onto both of the grips and supporting her body horizontally in the air over her elbows. The longest she'd ever managed to hold the "killer" for was two

strides, but on this magnificent morning when anything and everything seemed possible, she managed to hold it for four.

"*¡Estupendo!*" her grandfather cheered, once she was back in a seat astride.

Then Adela heard applause. She glanced toward the barn where the sound of clapping was coming from and saw Mr. McFarland with Daphne. Daphne was wearing her light blue leotard.

Why were they here? Daphne's next lesson wasn't until the following afternoon.

Adela did a simple dismount to the outside. The second her feet touched the ground, Daphne ran into the circle.

"I want to try that!" she cried.

Abuelito shook his head and halted Rio.

"It's getting hot out here, and he's had enough of a workout already," Abuelito said to Daphne. "Besides, your coach, Isabel, isn't around," he went on. "She's over at the Conovers' stable, practicing with the Flying Angels."

"I know. We just stopped by to pick up my gym bag," Daphne said.

She seemed a little put out that Abuelito wasn't letting her vault.

"Feel free to use one of the practice barrels,

though," Abuelito added helpfully.

Mr. McFarland walked over to Adela on the far side of the ring. "That was just wonderful!" he said to her. "Are you planning to use those exercises at the Alamo Festival in San Antonio?"

Adela opened her mouth to reply, but Daphne answered for her. "She's won't be in the festival, Dad. Don't you remember what happened to her in Austin?" she said. "Adela's not even a Flying Angel anymore."

Adela glared at Daphne, suddenly furious. Even though what Daphne had said was true, she still didn't want Daphne McFarland speaking for her!

Before she could say so, though, her grandfather said, "Here come your sisters."

The yellow Volkswagen was barreling up the gravel road with all three of the Salinas girls inside. Diana pulled in beside the barn.

"Hey, Daphne!" Vicki yelled out the back window.

Isabel climbed out of the passenger seat and said, "Hi, Daphne. Hello, Mr. McFarland."

And Diana said, "Abuelito, we told Mrs. Conover we'd let the Flying Angels use Nina for a few days. Charlie has a sore back. May I borrow your truck to drive her over there?"

Diana's little car wasn't powerful enough to pull a couple of thousand pounds, which is what their horse trailer weighed with a horse inside it.

"Why don't you come with us?" Vicki said to Daphne. "After you watch us practice, maybe you could teach all of the Flying Angels a few new moves."

"I'd like that," Daphne said. "Is that okay, Dad?"

"We'll give her a ride home, Mr. McFarland," said Isabel.

"My truck's been acting up. I'd rather drive Nina over myself," Abuelito said to Diana. "Adela, keep me company."

But Adela shook her head.

Daphne and Vicki were having a hushed conversation. When Adela caught them both looking at her, they glanced quickly away.

Daphne must have told her I was vaulting this morning. Now I'll have to hear about it from Vicki, Adela thought.

But when the older Salinas girls came back to the house for lunch after practicing with the other Flying Angels, it wasn't Adela who was on Vicki's mind—it was Daphne McFarland.

"I knew Mrs. Conover was going to like her!" Vicki said.

She was setting five places at the kitchen table, for herself and her sisters and Abuelito.

"Going to like who?" asked Adela.

"As if I didn't know," she added to herself.

"Daphne," said Diana.

"She showed the team two new dismounts," said Isabel, pouring iced tea for everyone.

"I spoke to Mrs. Conover about Daphne trying out for the Flying Angels," Vicki said.

How can Daphne try out for the team? Adela asked herself. Even the beginners at the stable have been around horses more than she has!

"Mrs. Conover had a great idea," Vicki went on. "She said why not have Daphne do a freestyle exercise at the Alamo Festival, before the real competition starts."

"A few of the younger kids from the stable are going to do a demonstration, too," said Isabel, as they all sat down at the table.

Abuelito nodded. "That's a good idea—get them used to performing in front of an audience."

"And give the Flying Angels a chance to see Daphne in action. Her cousin will be there with the

Tyler team. Daphne's all excited about it. The only thing is"—Vicki turned to look at Adela—"she'd really like to borrow Rio for the show."

"Rio?" said Adela, taken completely by surprise.

"Is that a problem? The coliseum's just a few miles down the road, and Abuelito can haul Rio home as soon as Daphne's done," said Vicki. "Is it because you're vaulting again? Is that why you don't want to loan Rio out?"

"Vaulting again?" Diana turned in her chair to face Adela. "You are? That's great, Adela!"

Adela shook her head. "I was just fooling around this morning," she said, glaring at Vicki. "I'm not vaulting seriously."

"So then it's okay if Daphne uses Rio at the San Antonio show?" Vicki asked, pinning her down.

Adela, not able to think of an answer that wouldn't make her seem totally selfish, reluctantly agreed.

"Abuelito, you wouldn't mind driving Rio over there, would you?" Vicki went on.

"No. I'm going anyway, to watch you girls," Abuelito said.

"Good," said Vicki, serving herself a big helping of fresh tomato and avocado salad. "I'll call Daphne right after lunch and let her know she has the horse."

Adela Helps Out

For the next two weeks Rio hardly seemed to belong to Adela.

Daphne McFarland was constantly at the Salinases' house, and she vaulted on Rio nearly every day. Whenever Adela wanted a chance to ride or vault, Rio was busy.

So was Isabel—busy coaching Daphne so that she would put on a perfect performance at the Alamo Festival.

Diana was the only one of her sisters who seemed to notice how difficult it was for Adela to have Daphne taking over her horse—and their house, for that matter. Daphne and Vicki were inseparable. They were always in each other's company.

Fortunately, Diana was good at coming up with things for Adela to do that got her away from the riding ring and the house.

One day she said, "I need another pair of arms and legs, Adela. I want to put together a knockout freestyle, because it's the last one I'll be doing with the team." She added, "We'll plan it out on the barn floor first, before I set it to music on horseback."

Diana drew a horse-size rectangle on the concrete floor of the barn, and she and Adela began working on a four-and-a-half minute freestyle for the eight Flying Angels to perform at the Alamo Festival.

"I hope everyone stays healthy," Diana said. "We haven't found a reserve vaulter yet."

She began to jot down notes in her vaulting notebook. "Okay. Isabel and I vault well together, and we're both strong, so we make good bases." She paired Numbers 1 and 3 in her notebook. "Amy is light enough to be a flier, and so is Vicki." She paired 2 and 5. "Sara Palmer knows ballet and can do excellent arabesques and splits."

Once Diana had listed all eight vaulters and their special talents, she and Adela tried out the routine on the floor of the barn.

"As Number 1, I'll vault on into a tuck, do a side

split for three canter strides, and then basic seat into a back lie, with my legs in the loops on the surcingle." As Diana spoke, she scribbled rapidly.

She went on. "Amy, as Number 2, will vault on over me. I'll grab her legs while she continues to hold onto the grips and push her into a handstand in front of me. She can hold the handstand for three strides. Then Isabel, as Number 3, will mount to the inside."

Diana put the cap back on her felt-tip marker. "Let's try it out so far," she said to Adela.

They worked on the freestyle routine for the rest of the afternoon. If the different moves didn't flow easily into one another on the floor, the girls adjusted them.

"If we have problems with the moves here in the barn," Diana said to Adela, "just imagine the trouble we'd have in a canter on Charlie."

Diana even included a couple of Adela's suggestions in the program: a direct mount into a zigzag for threes and a roll-off dismount for pairs.

When Diana was finally satisfied that every vaulter would be used to the best of her ability in the short time allowed, she wrote out the whole program as simply as possible. The next step would be for the Flying Angels to start practicing at the Conovers' stable. There they would practice the program with music.

A couple of days after the program was planned,

Diana insisted that Adela practice pairs with her on Rio.

"It might give me some additional moves for the freestyle," Diana told her.

With Abuelito as longeur, Adela did a shoulder sit on Diana's shoulders. Then they tried a skater's lift and then a shoulder flag.

Diana even stood on Rio's back and lifted Adela in a flying angel, the kur exercise from which the team took its name.

Once they'd vaulted off, Adela said excitedly, "That was awesome!"

"Yes, it was," said Diana. "I think you've sort of lost sight of the fact that vaulting is *fun*, Adela. And that's why I vault. I know the team can't win every competition, although it's nice when we do. But when I master a new move, or put together a beautiful freestyle, or just feel that I'm totally in sync with my horse, then I'm on top of the world. It just doesn't get any better." She smiled at her sister. "And it's fun being part of a team, too."

"Unless you let the team down," Adela said, ruefully.

"Adela, everyone has great moments and less-than-great moments," Diana said. "One day you might be having a hard time at a competition, while someone else on the team might be vaulting

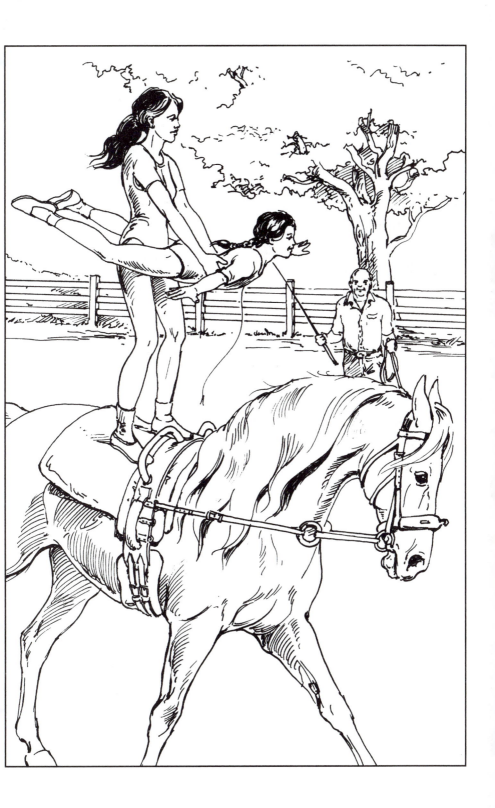

perfectly. It all balances out. As a member of a vaulting team, you should feel less pressure, not more."

She put her arm around Adela. "Anyway, I'm really glad you're vaulting again, even if it's only at home."

Adela was glad, too, but there was a problem: She wanted her own horse back.

Sometimes Adela felt like Daphne's exercise girl, hanging around just to warm Rio up and cool him off for the real vaulter. Daphne seemed to take it for granted that Adela would be the one to tend to Rio's needs. She never offered a hand when there was horse work to be done.

Adela knew her sisters would pitch in, but she wasn't comfortable leaving the care of her horse up to her sisters. The Andalusian was her responsibility.

One afternoon, a few days before the Alamo Festival, Adela was leaning against the paddock fence, watching one of Daphne's sessions on Rio. Isabel was the longeur as well as the coach.

Although it was late afternoon, it was still hot, and Rio was dark with sweat. But he continued to circle again and again in a relaxed canter, moving smoothly and loosely. It left Daphne free to concentrate on her exercises: a swing-around, a knee-jump with a half-turn, full splits.

It's like looking at a vaulting manual, Adela thought. She's flawless. And I have to give her full points for practicing as hard as anyone could.

In fact, it seemed as if Daphne would have been willing to vault endlessly, if Isabel hadn't called out, "That's enough for today, Daphne. Rio's been cantering for miles already."

"Oh," Daphne said, as though she'd forgotten all about the Andalusian beneath her.

She did a backward push-away dismount, and Isabel halted Rio, unclipped the longe line, and unhooked his reins.

"Whew! It's roasting. Do you want something to drink?" Isabel asked Daphne, handing her the reins.

"No, I'm going to put in some time on a practice barrel." Daphne, in spite of her intense workout, looked as fresh as when she started.

"Adela?" said Isabel.

"No, thanks," Adela said. Her sister headed toward Abuelito's house.

Daphne, leading Rio, walked over to where Adela was standing. She always turned the Andalusian over to Adela before she joined Vicki at the practice barrels.

Daphne usually never bothered to say much to her, so Adela was surprised when Daphne suddenly blurted out, "I want to ask you a favor, Adela."

"What?" she asked. She'd already lent Daphne her horse. She had nothing left to give.

"You'll be going to the Alamo Festival, won't you?" Daphne said.

Adela shrugged. She wasn't really looking forward to watching the Flying Angels perform without her. And she certainly wasn't looking forward to watching Daphne be the star of the show on *her* horse. But the Alamo Festival would be Diana's last competition as Number 1 vaulter for the team, and Adela didn't want to miss that. Besides, she wanted to see the Flying Angels perform the freestyle routine she and Diana had put together.

"Yes, I'll be there," she said to Daphne.

"Excellent!" said Daphne. "Can you and your grandfather help me out with Rio? Vicki and Isabel will be getting ready for the team performance, and I'm not so great at doing the horse stuff, as you know."

Before Adela had a chance to respond, a shriek came from the direction of the practice barrels.

Adela spun around. "It's Vicki!" she cried.

She could see her sister sitting on the ground between the barrels, rocking back and forth as if she were in pain.

Adela started running, with Daphne right behind her. By the time they reached Vicki, Isabel was already kneeling on the ground beside her sister, gently touching Vicki's right ankle.

"I was trying Daphne's 'flank-off over croup' dismount," Vicki said to Isabel, "and I landed wrong."

"Your ankle is puffy," Isabel said.

"I can't believe I did this!" Vicki cried. "What about the Alamo Festival? It's only four days away!"

Abuelito hurried up to them. "What's the commotion?" he asked.

After Isabel had filled him in, he took a quick look at Vicki's ankle.

"It may not be too bad," he said to Vicki. "Let's get you into the house fast. That ankle needs to be iced so that the swelling can go down."

He and Isabel linked arms to carry Vicki to the main house.

"I'll fill some plastic bags with ice," Adela said, also starting for the house. "Daphne, you'll have to untack Rio," she said over her shoulder. "And walk him around."

"Walk him?" Daphne said, as Adela broke into a run.

"Thirty minutes," Adela called back.

Isabel and Abuelito set Vicki gently on the living room couch and packed ice bags around her swelling ankle.

Adela poured her sister a soda and handed her the television remote. Then she went back outside to check on Daphne and Rio.

She spotted them at the far end of the barn. The surcingle and backpad were lying on the ground where Daphne had dropped them.

Daphne was leading Rio around and around in a tight circle, holding onto the tip ends of the reins so that she didn't have to get too close to the horse's feet.

"I untacked him," Daphne told Adela, eagerly holding out the reins for Adela to take.

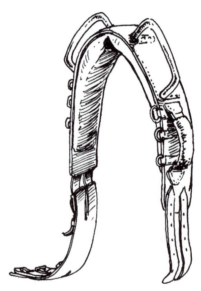

Adela bit her tongue, refraining from saying that dropping a sweaty surcingle and pad in the dirt means a lot of extra work cleaning them later on.

Adela patted Rio. How could Daphne have a clue about taking care of tack when Isabel and Vicki hadn't shown her how to do anything for a horse?

What would happen when Daphne was a member of the Flying Angels? Adela wondered. She smiled. Mrs. Conover certainly wouldn't cut Daphne any slack, not even if she was the best gymnast in the world. All of the Flying Angels took turns grooming Charlie, including the Number 1 vaulter.

And Charlie had enormous feet. How was Daphne going to like picking them up to clean out his hooves?

"Would you like me to teach you a new vault-on?" Daphne asked, waving toward the practice barrels.

"No, thanks," said Adela. "I'm going to walk Rio around some more."

"Then I think I'll go up to the house and see how Vicki is doing," said Daphne.

"How did I get us into this, Rio? It seems like you're Daphne's horse now and I'm the stablehand," Adela said, as she watched Daphne skipping up the front steps to the house.

The Andalusian nickered softly in response.

"I can promise you one thing, though," Adela told her horse. "After this weekend, Daphne is not going to be riding you. She can get her own horse."

The Big Day

The Salinas girls set their alarms for five o'clock on Saturday morning. Compulsory vaulting began at 10:30 at the Alamo Coliseum.

By the time the four of them sat down to breakfast, Diana, Isabel, and Vicki were already dressed in their light blue leotards, and their gym bags were packed with vaulting shoes, towels, and hairbrushes.

While the girls downed their breakfast, their mother examined Vicki's ankle.

"It still looks a little swollen to me," Mrs. Salinas said doubtfully.

"Absolutely not, Mom," Vicki said. "It's just fine. See how I can move it?" She held her right leg in the air and rotated her foot. "No pain at all."

"I think it'll be okay, Elena," their father said.

"We'll bandage it carefully before Vicki vaults," Abuelito said.

"Besides, I'd vault even if it did hurt. We no longer have a reserve," Vicki said, looking straight at Adela.

Adela spooned up some cereal, letting the remark slide.

"Not yet, anyway," Vicki added.

She was obviously thinking about Daphne, absolutely certain that her friend was going to blow everyone away at her vaulting debut that day.

Diana checked her watch.

"Almost six o'clock. The Conovers will have loaded up Charlie by now," she said to Isabel and Vicki. "I told Mrs. Conover we'd meet them at the coliseum to help warm him up."

"Adela, we'd better start working on Rio ourselves," said her granddad. "If the compulsories begin at 10:30, then the exhibitions will go on even earlier. Is Daphne coming here?"

"No, she's not," Vicki said. "She's riding over to

the coliseum with the Conovers."

Daphne acts like she's a full-fledged Flying Angel already, Adela thought.

But she had too much to do to waste time getting upset over Daphne. After all, Daphne wasn't the only one making her debut. For the first time, the Flying Angels would be seeing Rio in the ring at a show.

Adela and Abuelito dampened and plaited the Andalusian's mane and tail. Then Adela groomed Rio carefully while her granddad put the surcingle, backpad, and bridle in the back of his truck, along with the longe line and whip. Then he hooked up the Salinases' horse trailer.

"All ready to go," Abuelito said.

Adela gave Rio's neck and chest one last swipe with the body brush. "We're ready, too," she said.

Adela and Abuelito loaded Rio into the horse trailer, hooked the leather strap behind him to hold him steady, and closed the heavy trailer gate.

"Next stop, downtown San Antonio," Abuelito said, as they started up the gravel road in the truck.

Adela's parents waved to them from the front porch of the house. "We'll see you in a couple of hours!" her dad called out.

Abuelito turned onto the blacktop, and about thirty minutes later they were driving through the

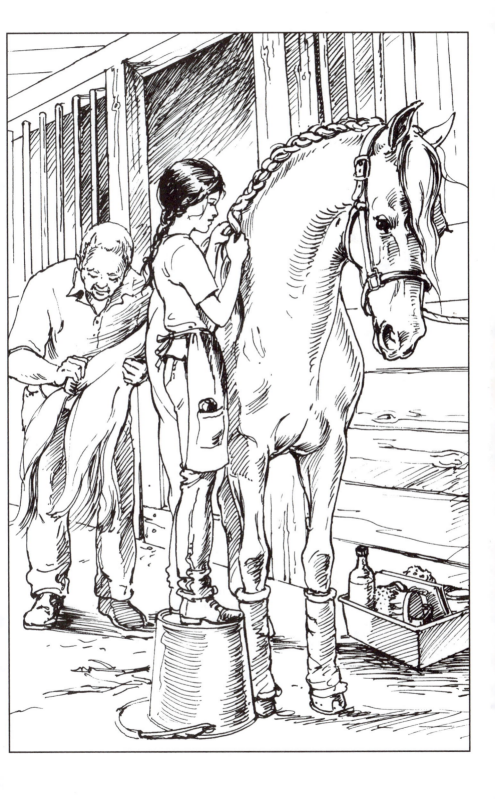

contestants' gate at the Alamo Coliseum.

Vaulting was just one of the events at the Alamo Festival. Adela saw trucks carrying cattle, sheep, and hogs, on their way to the livestock barns for judging, and a collection of old tractors, gathered for the vintage tractor pull.

Adela knew there were other riding events scheduled for that Saturday as well, such as reining, barrel racing, and pole bending.

But when Abuelito pulled into the parking area near the outdoor practice rings, there were vaulters everywhere. Vaulters were leading horses around, or tightening surcingles, or warming up by running in place.

Adela saw the Delmar Dusters in their gold leotards stretching to limber up their leg muscles. The Valley Girl Vaulters in their white leotards with purple stripes were doing handstands and forward rolls. Then she spotted the light blue leotards of the Flying Angels, gathered near the Conovers' trailer.

"One, two, three, four . . .," Adela counted leotards, just to make sure that all eight of the Flying Angles had made it to the competition. ". . . five, six, seven, eight . . . nine?" she exclaimed.

"No, eight Flying Angles, and Daphne," Abuelito said, opening the truck door. "She's standing next to the girl in the green leotard."

Daphne, wearing her short-sleeved light blue leotard, was talking a mile a minute to an older girl dressed in a sea-green leotard whose reddish-brown hair was wound in a braid around her head.

"Hi, Adela!" Diana called out.

Daphne heard her and turned around. When she caught sight of Abuelito about to unload Rio, she grabbed the girl in green by the arm and pulled her toward the truck.

"Hey, Adela," Daphne said when she was close enough. "This is my cousin Meredith."

Adela nodded politely at the girl, who returned the greeting.

"And this is the horse I'm riding," Daphne said to Meredith, pointing to Rio as he backed out of the Salinases' trailer.

Rio was trying to take everything in at once as he investigated his new environment. His eyes focused on one thing for a second or two, and then another. His ears twitched as he took in deep breaths full of unfamiliar smells.

"He's beautiful," Meredith said to Adela.

"Thanks," said Adela. "I think so, too."

"It's really great of you to let Daphne use him," Meredith added, reaching out to pat Rio's neck.

After the introductions, Daphne had barely given the Andalusian a second glance. "I've come up with some very cool moves!" she told her cousin. "I can't wait for you to see me in the ring."

Meredith said, "I can't wait, either."

Adela thought Meredith seemed like a nice person who actually knew something about horses. She'd already paid more attention to Rio in five minutes than Daphne had in weeks.

"How old is he?" Meredith asked Adela.

"Thirteen," Adela said. "But I've had him less than a year. He belonged to Talia Weston; she's a famous vaulter from West Texas. Have you heard of her?"

Meredith shook her head. "Daphne told me you've given up performing after what happened in Austin," she said to Adela, still stroking the horse. "But I'm sure you realize that everyone has off days. It's all part of the sport, or part of any sport, for that matter."

"Don't say that, Meredith. It'll be bad luck for me!" Daphne teased. "I'm planning on never having an off day."

Adela figured that Daphne was counting on her to get the Andalusian tacked up; on Abuelito to be the excellent longeur he always was; and on Rio to automatically perform his part. Then Daphne would run into the ring and vault perfectly, just as she did on the practice barrel back at the ranch.

And then she'd be a Flying Angel.

"Aunt Virginia and Uncle Bill are here!" Meredith said suddenly.

She and Daphne waved to Daphne's parents, who were standing together at the far side of the practice rings.

"Shouldn't I start warming up?" Daphne asked Adela.

"I guess so," Adela said.

"And I'd better join the rest of my team," Meredith said. "Good luck with your demo, Daphne. Nice to meet you, Adela."

While Daphne limbered up, Adela tacked up Rio. Then she led him to one of the three practice rings. Abuelito followed with the longe line and whip.

The Delmar Dusters were vaulting in the ring to the right. To the left were the girls of Meredith's team in their sea-green leotards.

Daphne walked over to the practice ring with her parents.

Mrs. McFarland seemed anxious about her daughter's upcoming performance. "I haven't watched Daphne vault up till now," she said. "I'm embarrassed to admit it, but I'm somewhat afraid of horses. They're so . . . so big."

"Rio is very gentle," Adela reassured her, patting the Andalusian's shoulder. "And he's been a vaulting horse for years."

Abuelito attached the longe line to Rio's bridle and led him to the center of the practice ring.

Adela stood on the sidelines beside the McFarlands and watched while Abuelito longed the horse for a few minutes with loose side reins to warm him up. Then he brought the horse to a halt and tightened the side reins.

"Everyone ready?" he asked.

Daphne smiled self-confidently at her parents and nodded yes.

Abuelito signaled Rio with the whip. The Andalusian moved away from the center of the ring and began to canter in a circle to the left, smoothly and evenly.

CHAPTER
TEN

Adela to the Rescue

Daphne trotted into the ring to stand behind Abuelito.

Then she ran down the longe line in step with Rio's canter, reached for the grips on the surcingle, and vaulted onto the horse into a shoulder stand.

Adela, outside the ring with Daphne's parents, heard Mrs. McFarland gasp and Mr. McFarland say, "Don't worry so much, Virginia. Daphne knows what she's doing."

Daphne lowered herself into a seat astride Rio. Then she began her compulsories: first the basic seat, which she held for five strides.

"I must agree that she certainly does look

wonderful on the horse," Mrs. McFarland said proudly.

To Adela, it was *Rio* who looked wonderful. His gray coat gleamed; his neck curved forward and slightly downward; he carried his tail proudly. He took smooth, even strides, his hind feet stepping precisely into the tracks of his front ones.

Daphne did a perfect flag, kneeling on her left leg and holding her left arm and right leg high in the air.

Next she performed a graceful mill.

Adela noticed that groups of vaulters were gathering around the practice ring, watching Daphne go through the compulsories.

Or maybe they were watching Rio, because Adela overheard a Delmar Duster saying to a teammate, "Her horse is excellent! I think he's an Andalusian. I haven't seen him before, have you?"

"No, but there's no way this horse hasn't competed," said the second girl.

Adela figured that Daphne would complete the rest of her compulsories as successfully as the first three. It was time for her to do Adela's favorite, the stand.

But instead of a regular stand, jumping from a basic seat to her knees, and then to her feet, Daphne tried a move that Adela had only seen her perform on the practice barrel.

Daphne swung her legs forward and backward, pushing herself lightly onto her knees. Then she turned loose of the grips on the surcingle.

"What's she doing?" a vaulter murmured.

Daphne balanced on her knees with her arms stretched out to the sides for several strides.

Then she gathered herself and actually managed a knee jump—that was a jump with a half turn—from her knees to her feet, ending up facing backwards on the horse.

But Daphne landed hard on Rio's spine—much too hard.

The horse flinched from the sudden pain, and he overstepped. He stumbled just slightly, but the brief bobble was enough to cause Daphne to lose her balance.

As she fell backwards, she grabbed for the left grip on the surcingle, missed, and caught instead the loop on the left side of the surcingle.

Daphne was now hanging upside down, with her heels barely hooked over Rio's back and her head only inches away from his cantering hooves.

Adela knew that if Abuelito were to stop Rio quickly, Daphne might very well fall on her head and neck, which was the most dangerous kind of vaulting accident. However, if Rio cantered much farther,

Daphne's heels would certainly slip, and she would slide beneath his hooves.

Adela rushed into the practice ring. As she ran toward Rio on the outside, she hoped he wouldn't shy away from her.

She grabbed the grips and vaulted onto the Andalusian from the right, into a push-up, so that she wouldn't bump Daphne's feet and dislodge her.

Adela hopped to her knees, then swung her legs down carefully until she was sitting astride Rio's croup.

She turned loose of the left grip, reached down with her left hand, and grabbed for Daphne's free right arm.

"Hold on," she said. "I've got you. You're safe."

As Adela pulled Daphne up, Abuelito slowed Rio.

When Daphne was safe, sitting sideways on the Andalusian, with Adela holding her on from behind, Rio halted.

Adela sat there and waited until her pounding heart slowly return to normal. Then she leaned toward Daphne and said, "Let me help you down."

Daphne turned her head to stare at Adela, white-faced. "He almost killed me!" she yelled. "Your stupid horse almost killed me!"

"He was hurt!" Adela exclaimed.

But Daphne had already pushed herself off, landing on the ground on Rio's far side.

Daphne's parents rushed over to her. Her mother was crying almost uncontrollably.

"This is an insane sport, and I won't have you doing it!" Mrs. McFarland said to her daughter through her tears.

Mr. McFarland was so angry his face was dark red. "This horse is totally unreliable!" he thundered at Adela as she dismounted. "The fact that your family put Daphne on a dangerous animal like this was completely irresponsible."

Adela backed up till she felt Rio's sturdy side behind her, and she leaned against him. It had been an accident. Rio wasn't at fault. In fact, if anyone was at fault, it was Daphne. She should never have tried out a new routine without telling anyone. She could have been seriously hurt.

Adela wanted to tell Daphne's parents all this, but she couldn't find the words. As Mr. McFarland continued to yell, she felt tears rising and then, suddenly, Abuelito was there.

"Our only mistake was letting a girl who knows and cares nothing about horses take part in a sport that is all about horses!" he told Mr. McFarland. "Believe me, this horse has years of vaulting experience behind him. He knows what he's doing! And so does Adela. In case you haven't realized it yet, she just saved Daphne from a very serious fall, brought on by your daughter's grandstanding!"

Mr. McFarland glared at Abuelito and his lips quivered, but he did not respond. Instead, he took his daughter and wife by the arm and led them away from the ring, toward the parking area. As they walked away, Adela overheard Daphne say to her parents, "At least Meredith didn't see me fall!"

A girl in a purple leotard came up to Adela. "That was an amazing move you made," she said. "What team are you on?"

"I'm not on a team," Adela said.

"Maybe you'd like to join ours," said the girl with a smile. "You and your horse." She reached out to pat Rio's shoulder.

Then Adela's sisters ran over to her, worry etched on their faces.

"What happened, Adela?" said Isabel. "We heard there was an accident over at one of the practice rings."

"You're pale," Diana said to her youngest sister. "Is everything okay?"

"And where's Daphne?" asked Vicki. "I saw her go off with her mom and dad, and she seemed really upset. Her parents seemed upset, too."

Abuelito said, "Give Adela a break, girls. She just saved your little gymnast from falling on her head, and the only response she got was Mr. McFarland jumping down her throat."

"Oh, really?" said Diana, her eyes flashing. She spun around, trying to spot the McFarlands through the multicolored throng of vaulters. "We'll just see about that!"

"He has no business saying anything to you!" Isabel declared. "If Mr. McFarland has a problem, he'd better talk to me. I am Daphne's coach, after all!"

"It's okay," Adela said, feeling good that her sisters were ready to stick up for her.

"You *were* Daphne's coach," Abuelito said to Isabel. "I think her parents will be putting an end to Daphne's vaulting career."

Isabel shrugged. "Oh, well," she said. "What's done is done. I'm sure I'll pick up another student before too long."

Only Vicki sounded disappointed. "I thought Daphne would make a great Flying Angel," she said. "She knows so much."

"Maybe about gymnastics, but nothing about horses," said Abuelito. "Why aren't you girls over there warming up?" he asked the three of them.

"Charlie had a loose shoe," said Isabel. "We're waiting for Mr. Conover to fix it."

Suddenly Sara Palmer, the Flying Angels' Number 4 vaulter, appeared. "It's not a shoe after all," she told them breathlessly. "Charlie strained a tendon!"

"Oh, no!" Isabel groaned.

"Is it serious?" asked Diana.

"He'll be okay, but Mr. Conover said we can't use him for several weeks," Sara replied glumly.

"What about riding Nina?" said Vicki.

"We can't drive home, load Nina into the trailer, and drive her back here, groom her, and warm her up, all before 10:30," said Diana. "We'll just have to forfeit."

Diana sighed.

Adela knew that this was Diana's last opportunity to vault with the Flying Angels. Moreover, the new freestyle program they had worked on together was going to be over before it even started.

"Why forfeit?" said Abuelito. "You've got the best vaulting horse anyone could want right here."

"Rio!" Adela said proudly, knowing immediately what her grandfather meant.

"Would you mind, Adela?" Diana said.

Adela shook her head. Watching Rio in the practice ring, she realized how he loved to perform.

"We still have almost an hour before the compulsories start," said Diana, taking Rio's reins from Adela. "Sara, run and get all the Flying Angels together. We'll try Rio out right now."

CHAPTER
ELEVEN

Rio Joins the Flying Angels

Watching each of the Flying Angels run through a few of their compulsories on Rio made Adela so proud she thought she would burst.

With Mr. Conover as longeur, Diana vaulted on, did a scissors, and a backward push away dismount. Amy Conover did a mill and a stand. Isabel did a flank, landing perfectly.

"The only thing better would be having you out there, too, Adela," said Abuelito. He was standing on the sidelines with Adela and her mom and dad, who had just arrived.

"It's Vicki's turn," Mrs. Salinas said after Sara Palmer did a cartwheel off.

Vicki vaulted on into a handstand, like one of Daphne's. Then she lowered herself into a basic seat, swung into a kneeling position, and did a flag.

When Vicki vaulted off, she seemed to favor her bandaged ankle, though she smiled at her parents and ran out of the ring as if everything was just fine.

"Do you think her ankle is still bothering her?" Mrs. Salinas asked worriedly.

Mr. Salinas said, "I don't believe a little twinge would stop Vicki today."

After all of the Flying Angels had had a chance to warm up, Mr. Conover brought the horse to a halt, not wanting to tire Rio out before the actual competition began.

Mrs. Conover joined the Salinas family. "Your Andalusian is a wonderful vaulting horse," she told Adela. "Thank you so much for sharing him with us today."

Adela smiled. Even if she herself wasn't part of the team, Rio would be.

Amy Conover and Sara Palmer started walking the Andalusian so that he wouldn't stiffen up, while Adela, her parents, and Abuelito hurried into the coliseum to find their seats for the show.

Adela glanced around, trying to spot Daphne. Maybe she had decided to stay. After all her cousin Meredith was vaulting today. After a careful search, though, Adela realized that Daphne didn't appear to be anywhere in the audience.

After the three vaulting judges had taken their places at the edge of the arena, the announcer said, "Welcome to the Fourth Annual Alamofest Vaulting Classic, ladies and gentlemen. The first team in the compulsory section of the competition is . . . the Delmar Dusters and their horse, Sassy!"

The team's run-in music played, and their longeur, a tall woman with short gray hair, jogged into the arena leading a light-chestnut Percheron who resembled the Flying Angels' Charlie.

The nine vaulters on the team followed them in. After the team had saluted the judges, the music changed, and the compulsory program began.

The Delmar Dusters were good, particularly at their mounts and dismounts. One girl, the Number 3 vaulter, did an amazing shoulder stand flip-off at the end of her compulsories.

"She'll get high marks," Adela's dad said over the applause.

After the Delmar Dusters had left the arena, the Valley Girl Vaulters trotted in. Their team was newer, the vaulters younger and amateurish. Even their horse, a bay gelding named Conan, looked rather inexperienced.

Several of the girls couldn't hold their position in the flag for the required four strides.

One girl slid all the way off the horse while she was attempting the mill, and had to vault back on to finish.

Although they all did well with the stand, two girls lost their grip in the scissors.

And one of the younger girls landed flat on her rear in the dirt when she vaulted off at the end of her flank.

Adela was afraid the girl might cry, but instead she scrambled to her feet, smiled at the judges as she brushed herself off, and got out of the way of the next vaulter.

The Tyler High-Flyers were a very different story. Their vaulting horse was a big Appaloosa named Bright Star, the only Appaloosa at the show. He was beautifully turned out. Every inch of him gleamed.

Most of the Tyler vaulters were older girls, probably at least fourteen and up. The Number 1 vaulter was Daphne's cousin Meredith, and she was excellent.

Not only could Meredith perform each of the

compulsory exercises perfectly, she also had a real feeling for her horse, always moving in harmony with him and never losing his rhythm.

Meredith was powerful—her exercises had terrific height—and she was also graceful.

Adela thought she'd probably get high marks from the judges, and she deserved them.

When Meredith vaulted off Bright Star, she got a huge round of applause from the audience.

Someone even yelled, "Way to go, Meredith!"

The voice sounded familiar. Adela turned in her seat and saw Daphne McFarland, still wearing the light blue leotard, sitting with her mother and father about thirty feet away from the Salinases.

Adela nudged her grandfather and pointed out Daphne to him.

Abuelito nodded. "I saw them," he said. "And I give Daphne credit for staying. I figured she'd go straight home in a huff."

Soon it was the Flying Angels' turn.

"The next team is from our area, and I'm sure many of you have seen them perform," the announcer said. "Please welcome the Central Texas Flying Angels and their vaulting horse, Rio!"

Adela was glad Mrs. Conover had taken the time to let the announcer know about the change in horses. It was wonderful to hear Rio's name over the loudspeakers.

When Mr. Conover trotted into the arena leading Rio, Adela gasped. Her Andalusian looked so impressive! Rio's ears were pricked forward. He held his neck and head alertly as he lifted his feet in time to the Flying Angels' music. He truly seemed happy to be back in the ring at a show.

With Diana carrying the whip, the eight vaulters in their light blue leotards were lined up behind Rio, moving in step with him. The whole group circled past all three judges.

Mr. Conover halted Rio in the middle of the ring, so that he faced the senior judge. The team saluted the judge. Then Diana remained in the center of the ring with the longeur and the vaulting horse, while the other girls ran to the side of the arena.

The Flying Angels' compulsory program was underway.

Adela soon realized that it was hard choosing between watching her horse and watching the team. But she paid close attention to her oldest sister's compulsories. Diana's exercises were as skillful as Daphne's cousin's, and Adela thought the movements flowed into one another even more smoothly than Meredith's had.

Maybe that was partly because Adela's horse cantered so smoothly and evenly. Rio would help anyone do her best that day.

Amy Conover and Isabel both completed their compulsories with no defaults that Adela could pick out.

Adela thought Sara Palmer waited a little too long between the first phase of the scissors and the second, but she didn't seem to make any other mistakes.

Then it was time for Vicki's compulsories. Mrs. Salinas clutched Adela's hand and didn't let go.

Vicki's ankle didn't seem to be bothering her at all through the vault-on or the basic seat. She managed the flag and the mill just fine. But when she hopped into a crouch for the stand, Adela saw Vicki wobble, as though her ankle was beginning to hurt.

Adela happened to glance toward Daphne, and noticed she was half out of her seat, a concerned look on her face.

Adela crossed her fingers as Vicki vaulted off Rio after completing her last exercise. When she landed, Vicki managed to maintain her balance, but she leaned slightly to the left, clearly favoring her right leg.

Daphne was now standing up, staring down at Vicki with an uneasy frown on her face.

When Vicki ran out of the ring toward the waiting Flying Angels on the sideline, Adela's mom said, "She's limping badly, Manuel."

Adela's dad nodded, and said firmly, "She's withdrawing from the competition, as of right now."

As the Number 8 vaulter, Allison Martz, was finishing her last compulsory, Diana dashed back into the ring to stand just behind Mr. Conover.

She took the whip from him as he slowed Rio down to a walk, and then to a halt.

Then the rest of the team ran into the ring as well, to line up beside Rio, Mr. Conover, and Diana. Vicki was limping.

The Flying Angels saluted the senior judge, and the whole group left the arena in order. Vicki had a hard time just keeping up.

"We'd better go take a look at Vicki," said Abuelito.

By the time Adela, her parents, and granddad had made their way out of the building to the practice area, Mrs. Conover had Vicki sitting on a bale of hay with her right leg up. She unwound the bandage around Vicki's ankle.

"Definitely swelling," Mrs. Conover said, looking at it closely. "You and Charlie will both need a couple of weeks to recuperate from your injuries."

"I'll be fine, Mrs. Conover," Vicki said. "I'll stay off my ankle for the next couple of hours. I'll pack it in ice."

"Victoria, are you trying to do serious harm to yourself?" Mr. Salinas asked. "You will not be vaulting this afternoon. I'm sorry," he said to the other Flying Angels, who had all gathered around Vicki.

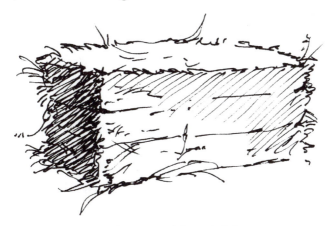

"That's okay," Diana said quickly. "Don't worry about it, Vicki," she told her sister. "I can rewrite the freestyle a bit, so that we only need seven girls for it, and . . ."

Then Diana caught sight of Adela and stopped herself. "Unless . . . ," she added.

"Unless what?" asked Martha Woller, the Number 6 vaulter.

Adela and her oldest sister gazed at each other for several seconds.

Adela shrugged. "I'll do it," she said at last.

"Adela already knows the freestyle," Diana said to the rest of the team. "We still have *eight* Flying Angels!"

"That's a terrific idea!" Mrs. Conover said.

Abuelito gave Adela a big hug.

Vicki glanced up at her little sister from her seat on the bale of hay. Then she smiled warmly and said, "You're a good sport. I'm glad you're stepping in, Adela."

She sounded relieved.

Mr. and Mrs. Salinas looked pleased.

"I don't have a leotard or shoes, though," Adela said.

She was trying to stick to practical matters, so that she wouldn't come down with a major case of stage fright, or start replaying her first dismal performance at a competition.

"I have a spare pair of vaulting shoes with me that you can use," said Sara Palmer. "You and I both wear size 5, right?"

"And I brought a second leotard along. It's in my gym bag," said Emily Bonner. "It might be a little too large for you, though."

Then another voice spoke hesitantly from the edge of the group: "Adela, I've got an extra leotard

that should fit you, and it's light blue."

"Daphne!" said Vicki.

Daphne McFarland smiled a little sheepishly at the Salinas girls. "I wanted to see how you were doing," she said to Vicki. "You were really limping out there."

Diana said to Adela and the rest of the Flying Angels, "We should run through the freestyle routine a couple of times."

"My clean leotard's in Mrs. Conover's car," Daphne told Adela.

"Thanks," Adela said, turning toward the parking area.

"Hey, Adela, wait a second," Daphne called out.

Adela stopped, and Daphne walked toward her.

"I did land on Rio too hard," Daphne said. "It wasn't his fault. He's a wonderful vaulting horse." She looked down at the ground. "You saved me from getting hurt, and I just want to thank you now, properly."

"You're welcome," said Adela.

"I also wanted to tell you that I've realized horses are not for me," Daphne said.

"But you have the potential to be such a good vaulter, Daphne," Adela said, and she meant it.

Daphne shook her head. "A good gymnast, maybe. *"You're* the Flying Angel, Adela."

106

Adela Flies Again!

The next couple of hours sped by for Adela.

After she had changed into Daphne's leotard and Sara's spare pair of vaulting shoes, she joined the rest of the Flying Angels at the practice barrel.

Adela was familiar with the Flying Angels' new freestyle because she'd worked on it with Diana the week before. But now she would have a serious part to play in it herself, taking Vicki's place as the Number 5 vaulter.

She also had Rio to worry about.

Adela had practiced several pairs movements on him in the past few months with Isabel and Diana, just for fun. But since she'd had him, Rio hadn't carried three girls on his back at the same time. Adela hoped her Andalusian had had plenty of experience with pairs and threes when he belonged to Talia Weston.

Mrs. Conover must have been thinking the same thing, because she said, "Girls, after you've run through the freestyle on the practice barrel, I want you to try out a few of the exercises on Rio, just to see how well he accepts the weight of two and three girls."

Adela hoped the upcoming freestyle event would go smoothly. According to the rules, their routine, set to suitable music—the Flying Angels had chosen a classical piece, with trumpets and French horns—had to be completed in under five minutes.

Time, however, was not the only concern. In a successful freestyle, a team had to perform various exercises at all heights on the horse, facing in all directions, and using one, two, and three vaulters. The horse was never to be left empty.

Also, the team's movements were supposed to flow easily together, and the girls' weight had to be evenly distributed on the horse's back, so that the animal never felt uncomfortable.

There were two hundred fifty recognized moves in the freestyle event, graded by the judges as difficult, medium, or easy. And Adela knew that the vaulters would not be the only ones marked; the horse would be marked as well.

Diana interrupted Adela's thoughts. "Don't worry about Rio," she said, as if she were reading Adela's mind. "He'll do just fine. Let's focus on making sure we know our routine perfectly." She handed Adela several sheets of paper on which she had diagramed the program into ten groups.

As the other girls warmed up, Adela studied Vicki's part in the routine.

As strong and experienced vaulters, Diana and Isabel were in groups one, two, three. Diana dismounted in group four; Isabel, not until group seven.

Adela's eyes moved down the page, until she found her place as the Number 5 vaulter in group nine.

She would vault on from the outside of the horse, into a seat facing forward. The Number 2 vaulter, Amy Conover, would already be sitting backwards in front of the surcingle.

Adela would quickly stand.

Amy would grip Adela's right wrist with her right hand, and Adela would stretch her left arm toward Rio's tail, turning her head in that direction as well.

The two girls would then lean away from each

other to balance their weight on Rio's back and hold the position for three strides.

Amy would turn loose of Adela's hand, and Adela would stand just behind the surcingle, facing forward for three strides, while Amy dismounted. Adela would immediately kneel on her left knee, with her right foot on the surcingle, for three strides. Her arms would be stretched out in front of her to help with her balance.

She would stand again for three strides, then kneel down on her right knee. Martha Woller would mount into a kneeling position behind Adela, and they would both remain that way for three strides.

Adela would then take hold of the grips to make a bench. Martha would move closer to her and stand, while Adela did a flag for three strides.

Martha would sit on the bench—which meant Adela's back—for three strides, and then dismount.

The freestyle would end with Adela standing again, and then doing a clip dismount to the rear of the horse.

"What do you think?" Diana asked after Adela had gone over the diagrams a few times.

"I think I can do it," Adela replied.

"Of course you can!" said Diana.

Mrs. Conover nodded. "Absolutely. Let's run through it, with music, on the practice barrel," she said.

The practice went smoothly. No one slipped or fell, and Mrs. Conover said that they were working well together as a team.

"If somebody falls," Mrs. Conover told the Flying Angels, "the vaulter left on the horse should improvise movements until that girl gets back on, or until her teammates start the next group of exercises."

Mr. Conover and Abuelito had been walking Rio around. Now the Flying Angels took over a practice ring. Everyone watched while Diana and Isabel vaulted on. Then Sara vaulted on and moved into a handstand between Adela's two sisters. Rio's canter remained as smooth and even as when a single person was performing a simple basic seat.

"Try a triple arabesque," Mrs. Conover called out.

She told Mr. and Mrs. Salinas and Adela, "This will be a good test of Rio's willingness to carry three girls, because he'll have the weight of one girl on each of his sides, plus a girl on his back."

Diana slipped her left foot into the left loop of the surcingle; Isabel, her right foot into the right loop, and they extended their opposite legs. Sara stood on Rio's back between them, raising her right leg and left hand. All three girls were perfectly poised.

Rio never faltered, continuing to canter as easily as before.

Adela, Abuelito, and everyone else standing near the ring broke into applause.

"We've got a winner here!" Mr. Conover called over his shoulder.

After the practice run, Mrs. Conover insisted that each of the Flying Angels take the time to drink some water and eat a protein bar for energy.

"If I ate a real meal right now, I would definitely get sick," Adela admitted.

By the time it was two o'clock, and the freestyles were about to begin, Abuelito and Adela's parents headed into the coliseum. Vicki hopped along beside them.

The rest of the Flying Angels waited in a line outside the building with Mr. and Mrs. Conover, while first the Delmar Dusters and then the Valley Girls Vaulters performed their programs.

When the announcer's voice boomed, "The Central Texas Flying Angels and their horse, Rio!" Adela thought that she might keel over from the excitement.

As the girls jogged into the coliseum behind Mr. Conover and the Andalusian, Adela heard a couple of voices shouting, "Way to go, Flying Angels!" and "Looking good, Adela!" Right away she recognized them as belonging to Daphne McFarland and Vicki.

For Adela, the next few minutes were almost like watching a video being fast-forwarded: the team saluted, the Flying Angels' freestyle music filled the coliseum, Mr. Conover started Rio cantering in a circle to the left, and Diana ran to him and effortlessly vaulted on.

Adela waited breathlessly for her turn, while her older sisters did handstands and arabesques.

Then Diana dismounted, running back to the sidelines and standing with Adela. Group four went well, as did group five. More groups performed. In what seemed like the blink of an eye, Diana was patting Adela's shoulder and whispering, "Good luck!"

For the second time that day, Adela vaulted onto Rio from the outside. Amy grinned encouragingly at her from her backward seat in front of the surcingle. Adela hopped into a crouch, and then she stood. Everything went so quickly that she hardly had time to think.

Amy reached for Adela's right wrist with her right hand, Adela stretched out her left arm, and the girls leaned away from each other. They were so perfectly balanced that Adela felt almost weightless.

Adela straightened up and Amy turned loose of her wrist and vaulted off. Adela stood for three strides, kneeled on one knee, stood again, then kneeled on the other knee as Martha Woller vaulted on behind her.

The two girls both kneeled for three strides. Then Martha stood, while Adela did a flag. They did the bench, and Martha vaulted off again.

Adela stood. For three strides, it was just Adela on her Andalusian in the middle of the ring at the Alamo Coliseum.

Adela took a deep breath, gathered herself, and did a high clip dismount back to earth, landing solidly, her arms outstretched, and a huge smile on her face!

There was loud clapping as Adela ran out of the ring to join the other Flying Angels.

There was no time for her to ask, "How do you think we did?" because Diana, with the other vaulters in a line behind her, had already started running toward Mr. Conover and Rio, both standing together in the center ring.

Diana took the whip from Mr. Conover, and everyone bowed to the senior judge.

The coliseum echoed with thunderous applause, and dozens of flashes from photographers' cameras went off in their faces.

Adela glanced over at Rio, a little nervous about how he might react to the noise and the lights, but the Andalusian behaved like a professional.

The freestyle was over.

The Flying Angels followed their longeur and vaulting horse out of the building, and the Tyler High-Flyers ran in.

Adela finally got to ask her teammates, "How do you think we did?"

But all of the girls were talking at the same time, not only about their own performances, but about how great Rio was.

Then Abuelito showed up, and he and Adela walked Rio around for half an hour, until they heard Isabel calling out, "Adela! Where are you?"

"Over here!" she replied.

"Bring Rio back. They're ready to announce the winners!" her sister said.

The Flying Angels waited outside the coliseum as the announcer named the third-place winners: "The Delmar Dusters and their horse, Sassy!"

"That was our rating last year," Emily Bonner reminded Adela.

All of the Flying Angels crossed their fingers as the announcer began speaking again: "The second place winners are . . . the Tyler Texas High-Flyers and their Appaloosa, Bright Star!"

"Maybe we'll win first," whispered Allison Martz.

"Maybe not," Martha Woller muttered uneasily. "The Canyon Hill Centaurs were excellent."

Just then the announcer's voice boomed from the loudspeakers, "And let's have a big hand for this year's Alamofest first prize winners . . . our very own Central Texas Flying Angels and their Andalusian, Rio!"

Excited chills ran up Adela's spine. Then Martha and Emily grabbed her, and the three of them started jumping up and down.

"We did it!" Isabel said, giving Amy Conover a high-five. "Our first blue ribbon in San Antonio!"

"What a great way to say goodbye to the team!" Diana exclaimed, hugging both of her sisters. "And we have you to thank for it, Adela!"

Adela smiled and reached up to pat her horse. "And don't forget Rio," she said. "We could never have won without him."

FACTS
ABOUT THE BREED

You probably know a lot about Andalusians from reading this book. Here are some more interesting facts about this striking European breed.

◠ Andalusians generally stand between 15.2 and 16.2 hands high. Instead of using feet and inches, all horses are measured in hands and inches. A hand is equal to four inches.

◠ Andalusians are usually gray. Sometimes they are bay (brown with a black mane and tail), brown, or palomino (gold with a white mane and tail).

◠ Andalusians have powerful hind legs and strong necks that are naturally arched. Their hooves are small and round.

∩ The face of the Andalusian is convex or straight. The forehead is broad, and the large eyes have an oval shape and a kind expression.

∩ The mane of the Andalusian is long, thick, and often wavy. The tail, too, is thick and lies close to the body when the horse is not moving.

∩ Andalusians come from Spain on the Iberian Peninsula. They get their name from a region of southern Spain where the horses are bred. The same horses are also bred in Portugal, but there they are called "Lusitanos."

∩ In Spain the Andalusian is called "Pura Raza Español" or "Pure Spanish Horse."

∩ Andalusians are one of the very oldest breeds. Cave paintings from 25,000 years ago depict horses that look very much like today's Andalusian.

∩ The Iberian cavalry was already riding Andalusian horses when the Phoenicians invaded, as early as 2,000 B.C.

∩ William the Conqueror (1027–1087), who became king of England, rode an Andalusian horse in the Battle of Hastings in the year 1066.

∩ In addition to being a very old breed, the Andalusian is an important breed. Many modern breeds of horse in both Europe and America trace back to Andalusian ancestors. In fact, almost every native breed in the U.S. can claim Spanish heritage, including Quarter Horses, Paints, Appaloosas, Mustangs, and Saddlebreds. The conquistadors first brought Spanish horses to the New World in the 16th century.

∩ In Europe scientific tests have proven that the Andalusian contributed to the development of the Connemara, the Cleveland Bay, the Friesan, the Hackney, the Percheron, the Thoroughbred, and the Welsh. The famous Lippizans also are descended from Spanish horses.

∩ The International Andalusian & Lusitano Horse Association (IALHA), which is located in Shoal Creek, Alabama, maintains a registry of purebred and half-bred Spanish horses. The IALHA, which is the world's largest Andalusian organization, also runs educational programs for owners, breeders, and judges to help them preserve and promote the traits of this classic breed.

∩ In addition, IALHA sponsors horse shows and clinics in breeding and judging Andalusians. The association publishes a bimonthly magazine and a Stud Book. They also maintain a website at http://www.andalusian.com.

∩ While the number of pure Andalusians continues to rise, half-bred Andalusians are also gaining in popularity. In the early 1970s, Mexican horse breeders crossed pure Andalusians with American Quarter Horses and called the resulting foals "Aztecas." The Azteca combines all the good qualities of both parents. They are elegant, strong, and sound, and they move with a ground-covering stride.

∩ Although Andalusians are expensive, their kind disposition and striking good looks make them good mounts for vaulting. In fact, Andalusians are so well behaved that even small children can handle them.

∩ Andalusians are well suited to dressage and other movements that require agility. Their natural gaits are muscular and controlled, as dressage demands. The "high school" maneuvers that the Lippizans have made famous were first practiced on Spanish horses in the 1600s. Today Andalusians excel at dressage, jumping, driving, and trail and pleasure riding under both Western and English tack. Andalusians also make handsome, high-stepping parade horses.

∩ Because of their innate "cow sense," Andalusians are great at Western activities such as roping and cutting. In their native Spain, these proud horses are still the mount of choice for bullfighting.